UNBOUND

A Novella

Ash Ericmore

Written by: Ash Ericmore

Copyright © 2020 Ash Ericmore

All Rights Reserved. This is a work of fiction. No part of this publication may be reproduced, distributed, or transmitted in any form or by any means, except in the case of brief quotations embodied in critical reviews.

ISBN: 9798848393309

CHAPTER 1

This wasn't the worst thing that had even happened to William. As he sat, his head being held back by the hair, with Tim Tollbridge standing over him, spit hanging from his mouth about to drop into his own, he thought back to last summer.

Last summer one of Tim's gang—his goons, call them what you will at sixteen and still in school—had cut William. Jason Lester was his name. He had cornered him outside of the school in a pathway that led down the side of the local allotments. Jason had pulled a knife and started waving it about. He'd thought it was funny. Even at the time, William didn't think that he had meant to use it. He was being the big man in place of the absent Tim. He was trying to frighten William. He'd said that he wanted to make William shit. He actually used those words. *I want you to shit.*

So William had lunged at him and punched him in the fucking face. His stupid, acne ridden, ugly fucking face. And William had laughed. A red patch grew from Jason's cheek where he punched him, like a fine merlot joining the dots of red on his stupid face. And once he'd started to laugh he couldn't stop. Jason lost his shit, and started to cry. The tears made William laugh harder. It was literally the funniest fucking thing.

That was, until Jason had lunged forward with the knife. Out of anger. He was unable to control his aggression. He punctured William just above the hip bone. It smarted like shit, and although William had lashed out with his fist again, this time not making contact, Jason pulled back, looked at the knife, and with a shocking realization that he had just stuck someone, dropped it and run. He had probably shit himself as well, but at the time, that wasn't William's main concern.

His main concern, understandably, was the blood that was gushing from him at an alarming rate. He applied pressure to the wound as he had seen in a variety of action-type films, but it hadn't seemed to help. Then there was screaming as other kids of varying ages had seen him, also on their way home from school. Then there was blackness.

That was the worst thing that had happened to him until this point. But not as bad as what was going to happen much later today.

Tim was holding back William's head by pulling hard on his hair with one hand and had a firm grip on his jaw with the other, holding it open. Then the gob dribbled from his mouth into William's. He could taste the tobacco on it, and it was weird and slimy.

Tim laughed and let William go, both his jaw and his hair.

William was sitting on one of the toilets in his local pub, *The George*. Sure, he was only seventeen now, but Cherry, the girl who worked behind the bar most lunchtimes gave him a bye. He was pretty sure she knew he was underage, but he was working an apprenticeship around the corner and had cash. He kept to himself most of the time and maybe, just maybe, she was sweet on him. She was older than him, but he'd always liked the look of her—in the few months he'd been coming here—and maybe one day he'd drink enough courage to ask her if she wanted to go out.

Tim turned to him. He had Jason and Del as back up. The two of them were stood behind Tim, by the door, making sure no one interrupted them. As it was lunchtime, the pub was pretty much deserted apart from William, Cherry, and the three of them, after they walked in.

No one was coming to help.

William had decided, as soon as they had followed him into the toilets, that it was best to let them do what they wanted, and get it out of their system. He'd heard on the grapevine that Tim had turned junkie after he left school and instead of moving on with his life and trying to make the best of having a shit school background and little in the way of qualifications, he had kept in with his old mates and they'd taken to doing small time criminal activity, instead of, you know ... working.

It had been months since he'd seen them. A few weeks since he'd even thought of them. And then there they were. The three fucking musketeers, standing in the doorway to his local while he was trying to chat up the bar staff.

Look at this, it's wanker.

He recognized the voice without turning to look, and there was a stabbing in his gut where he still had the scar. He glanced over his shoulder and saw that Jason was with them. He'd gotten into all sorts of shit over the stabbing, but the wonderful fucking British legal system had called it *assault*, not fucking attempted murder, and while he got in shit, he didn't do jail time. Jammy fucker.

"So." Tim smiled at William, sat in the cubicle, the door open. "You testified against my boy." He slapped Jason's chest with the back of his open hand. "He's only just got off community service. What are we going to do about that, grass?"

William shrugged. Hopefully Cherry would think something was amiss—all four of them being in the crapper at the same time for this long—and either come and find out what was what, or call the police. He just had to buy time. "Buy me a drink and respect my honesty?"

Tim stepped forward and slammed his foot down hard onto William's knees. The impact hurt less than the God-damned porcelain cutting into the back of his legs. He was wearing his work shorts. Working on the site—sunny today. "Cunt," William blurted without thinking. He covered his mouth with his hand and looked up at Tim. Tim had a look of surprise that morphed into anger pretty sharpish. He stepped forward and punched William. It knocked his head back, as everything went black. His shoulders cracked against the cistern, and the back of his head caught the wall. He could feel hot liquid on his face. Taste the iron, from the blood. He couldn't see, blinded by the impact, his nose jammed hard with blood. "The fuck?" he said, quietly, trying to keep composure.

Trying not to make everything worse. He braced himself, waiting for the worst. He couldn't defend himself, not against all three of them, blinded, and pissing blood.

In the back of his mind he had always suspected that this would happen one day.

"Come on then. Get it over with."

Tim giggled. "You think that we'd do anything here?"

Yes, William thought. *Yes, I do.*

"Fucker."

William held his eyes shut, and waited. He heard the door to the toilets open and close again and then he was in silence. He opened his eyes slowly, blinking away the tears. He still couldn't breathe through his nose. He looked down at himself. Blood covered his white work shirt. *Great.* That was going to need explaining. He rolled his tongue around in his mouth hoping none of his teeth were broken. It didn't feel like it. Touching his nose, he winched with pain, and jerked back. "Shit." Sitting for a moment, he wondered what to do next. Get up, he supposed.

He looked at himself in the mirror. He nose was bigger than it used to be, swollen, but not broken, he hoped. Washing the blood off his face made it look better, but not much.

There was a knock at the door.

William flinched, and turned to face the door. *Calm down*, he thought. *They'd hardly be knocking if they were back, now would they?*

The door creaked open a crack. "Will?" It was Cherry.

"Yeah," he responded, turning back to face the mirror.

The door didn't move. "You okay?"

"Come in," he said. There was no point in hiding from her. She was going to see him when he left the toilets, anyway.

Cherry pushed the door open and stood looking at him, her mouth open. "What the … did they … I'm calling the police." She turned to leave.

"No," William called her back. "It'll only make it worse."

She came back into the toilets and walked up behind him, putting her arms around him while he explained who they were.

After cleaning him up, and a pint on the house, William returned to work to explain why he was late, and why there was fucking blood all over him.

CHAPTER 2

William had worked the rest of the afternoon shift. Don, his foreman was a good sort, and had said he could go home if he wanted. Let his ma take a look at his face. William hadn't told him that he'd moved out a couple of months back because his ma was shacked up with this violent fucker that was hitting both of them. He declined, politely saying he was paid to work. In actuality he was shaken from meeting up with Jason more than Tim again and just wanted to be around people. Tim was a twat, sure, but Jason stuck him. Man, that still scared him.

Come five, the site closed down for the night and William left with everyone else. They were all heading back to the pub, it being Friday, but much as William would have normally taken the opportunity to sink a few with the rest of the guys, maybe see Cherry, he didn't feel like it tonight. He was going to stop at the Spar on the way home and get a four-pack of some cheap Eastern European lager that was in double figures, and get absolutely trousered.

Leaving site, he turned left, the rest of them turned right, and Don pulled out behind them in his four-by-four, locking the gate before taking off home to his family. He gave William a little wave as he drove past.

It was only a couple of miles home, and less if he took the alleyway that ran down the side of the railway line.

The one his ma had always told him to avoid.

William felt a little strange as he walked. He felt like someone was watching him. That feeling like déjà vu, but not. He crossed the front of the railway station and walked across the car park to the edge of the line. The alley ran from there, a mile up the road, almost to his flat. It was always quiet because it didn't really go anywhere.

William pushed his buds in his ears and took into the alley, blasting metal. He was only a little way in when he started feeling uncomfortable. Looking behind him the alley had curved slightly and he couldn't see the other end of it. On one side the fence that led into the train yard was thick and tall with blackberry bushes. On the other were the backs of old houses, no windows, just bricked up to stop the noise from the trains.

He picked up the pace.

He heard something beneath the music and reached into his pocket to turn off the player. Then something hit him from behind and he barrelled to the ground, turning onto his back as he did. There were the three of them. They were wearing masks, but he knew. *Of course it was them*. They hadn't even bothered to change their clothes since lunchtime.

They were all wearing Halloween clown masks. Scary fucking ones.

William looked at them. This was it. This was the kicking for putting his hands up in court and pointing at Jason. He scrabbled away from them into the bushes, trying to get a purchase to get himself back up onto his feet, but the thorns of the bush cut into him, stinging and drawing blood like a cat scratch. Tim was in the middle of the three of them. He was the one who had dropped William. It felt like he'd punched him in the kidneys. It made breathing hard, but fuck it. It was going to get worse.

Tim crouched down. He didn't speak, he just nodded.

William could see his eyes through the mask. He looked hungry. Thirsty. He looked like he was enjoying the thought of whatever he had decided to do next. Tim stood and held his hand out to William. He didn't see he had a choice, so William reached up and took it, and Tim hefted him back to standing. At the last second, he used William's weight and momentum against him, and as William was pulled back upright, Tim dug his fist into Williams's stomach, dropping him to the floor again.

The other two laughed.

William landed on his arse, rolling onto his side as he tried to get his breath. The two blows had knocked all of the wind out of him, and now his muscles hurt more than after just a day on the site. Tim kicked him. He couldn't defend himself. His boot went into William's stomach. He had his arms cradling there from the last punch, but it didn't stop the force reverberating through him. Then Tim kicked him in the face.

A flash of blackness.

William reached up as the blood gushed from his nose, again. He felt his lip had split, before everything started to feel strange, bloated. His face was swelling up. And other kick sent his head snapping back, another flash of blackness. He couldn't see anything out of his left eye. He couldn't open it.

William choked on his blood as it slipped and slid around in his mouth, down into his gullet, down the back of his throat. Hot. Sticky. Metallic. In quick flashes he saw Tim being congratulated by his friends. Was that it? Was this enough? William could see his hand reaching out towards them. He wasn't moving it. It was an unconscious, involuntary action. Pleading for help. Tim stepped forward and stamped down hard on his hand. He felt the movement, but no pain. No sound. Numb buzzing.

Jason and Del came around Tim, putting their arms somewhere on his body, and lifted William. The numbness subsided and things started to hurt. His hand, his fingers, he couldn't move them properly. Where they were holding him up, his ribs. Busted, maybe. He couldn't breathe properly.

They pushed his face into the bush. He didn't feel the thorns, just the overwhelming feeling of being drowned. Blood in his lungs. Face full of leaves. Mouth swollen.

He felt movement at his waist. Feeling around in his pockets? No. While the two of them held him, Tim was removing his belt. William felt the air go cold on his thighs as his shorts dropped to his ankles.

Panic washed over him, and William tried to get

his arms free, pushing and pulling on both sides at once, trying to free himself from the two men's grip. It earned him another hard strike in the kidneys from Tim. His legs went out from under him and he started to drop to the ground, but they held him. Hoisted him back up.

He felt Tim pull his underwear to the side.

No. He tried to cry out. He tried to move, but there was no strength in his fight, and no room to get words from his swollen lips.

Then he felt Tim enter him.

CHAPTER 3

William pulled his shorts up with one hand, still laying on the concrete. No one had come up the alley since it had happened. He wept. Got to his knees. He looked around the ground. There was blood. His. All of it.

Tim had done what he wanted and the three of them had left.

William got to his feet. He sniffed up blood. The little finger on his left hand was pointing in the wrong direction. He tried to close a fist, and couldn't. He held his shorts up, and started to limp towards his flat. He didn't think. He couldn't.

The numbness from the attack covered his whole body, not just where they'd hit him. Struck him. Touched him. It was everywhere. He continued to the corner of the alley, and looked around. There was no one in the small cul-de-sac that led from the alley to the main road. He didn't want to see anyone. He didn't want anyone to see him.

He limped across the street and up the three steps to the front door of the house. He fumbled in his pockets for the keys. It was only then that he realized that they hadn't taken anything of financial value from him. But *only* financial value. His wallet was still in his side pocket. His keys, now in his hand.

But they'd taken everything else.

He managed to get the keys into the lock and fell

through into the communal hallway. He grunted as he landed. His ribs kicking him back. His hand splitting in pain. William rolled his feet into the hall and kicked the door shut, and lay there for a few minutes. He tried to let the safety of the house wash over him, but he couldn't. It didn't. He got to his knees and crawled to the door to his flat, and found the lock with the keys, before flopping into that doorway too. He lay at the bottom of the stairs directly inside the front door for what felt like an eternity. He didn't want to move.

Eventually he found the strength—he didn't know where from—to climb the stairs. He took his clothes off and sat in the shower. The water washed the blood from him. It soothed his body. He sat with the warm water beating down on him for an hour, before he climbed from the shower and threw his clothes in the bin.

He felt his ribs tenderly. They may have been broken, maybe cracked. He pulled his bent fingers together with the other hand. Pain shot up his arm, into his shoulder. His chest. That made him call out which burned his ribs.

William collapsed to the sofa.

CHAPTER 4

SIX MONTHS LATER

"How did you get here?" Sebastian Noir spoke to Will without looking at him. The ink machine vibrated in his hand and he didn't let conversation break his concentration.

Will watched the ink going in. Sebastian was recommended by a friend of a friend of a friend. It had taken him far too long to get to this point, so hadn't wasted much time in the why's or wherefores as to the reasoning he needed specialized tattoos.

Sebastian was the only person in the country that Will had found willing to ink him with an ink, holy water, goat's blood mix. "Julie-Ann. A friend of Trish," Will replied.

"Trish the Goth?" Sebastian lifted the needle. "Wow. You do move in some circles."

Will nodded. He rested his head back.

"So, I mean, I get asked to ink with some strange shit. People's relative's ashes. The blood of their spouses. But this?" He put the machine back down onto Will's forearm. "And what do these symbols mean?"

"They're Enochian."

Sebastian nodded. Will knew that he didn't know

what they meant. Or what Enochian was, probably. That was just as well. He was fed up with everyone telling him what to do. He just wanted this done, and then he could move onto the next stage alone. For now.

"All done." Sebastian wiped the residue ink away and cleaned Will's arm. He looked at Will's other arm. Covered in religious utterances, the tattoo's on that arm didn't need to be inked with anything special. Bloke in Birchingate did it for fifty quid. "You into some voodoo, or what?"

Will nodded. "Yeah," he said quietly. "Something like that. What's the damage?"

"A hundred as agreed."

Will pulled his wallet from his leather jacket draped over the back of the chair and counted out six twenties. He tossed them into the chair he'd just left. "Keep the change." He swung the jacket over his shoulders and slipped his arms in.

"You want to be careful—"

"Gotcha," Will interrupted, ignoring the warning about infection that was coming. He unlocked the door to the shop and let himself out. The weather bit against him. Cold February weather. It was dark. The door closed behind him, and he heard Sebastian latch it. Will zipped up the jacket and thrust his hands into the pockets. One last stop to Trish, and he could head back home.

———

Trish sat on the floor at Will's feet. She had put a shock of white hair on the side of her head, perfectly stark against the black, since the last time he had seen her. She was running her fingers over his Enochian letters. "What do they say?" she asked.

"They're part of a spell," he answered. He lifted the joint to his lips, and sucked.

"To do what?"

"Magic," he answered.

She giggled. She'd had too much to drink. Stumbling to her knees she rested both of her hands on his legs. She was wearing a black lace dress thing. Black makeup over the eyes. Will casually stared at her. She was good looking. A bit skinny. But she was a free spirit, and that was attractive. She smiled at him, and Will knew what was coming next. She'd tried it several times over the last month, twice when she'd had too much to drink. "Are you gonna fuck me tonight?" she asked.

Will kept his eyes on hers. He could. She was his type. *Was*. He smiled, as warmly as he could these days. "No, darlin'. You know I'm not into that." He hadn't been into that for six months now.

"So what did you come back for?" She pouted and slumped back to the floor.

Will passed her the joint. "Here." He pulled three hundred quid from his back pocket and handed it to her. "For your help."

She nodded. "I still don't know if it's going to work."

"It will." He reached down and booped her nose. She passed back the joint and he took a toke, sitting back. It was time.

CHAPTER 5

Will sat on the floor of his living room. There was no furniture in the room anymore. No carpet. He sat on the bare floorboards and lit the final candle on the last point of the pentagram. He anointed it with the conjure bag that he'd purchased from a man called *Shack*, in Manchester three weeks ago.

"Belphegor," he said, merely a whisper. "Belphegor, come to me."

In the centre of the pentagram, a circle of dark liquid started to form. Will breathed in sharply. The pool spread, first the size of a saucer, then a tea plate. Soon it was the size of a dinner plate. The viscous red liquid brought a smell of iron with it.

Then a ripple appeared from the centre. The pool continued to gain in size as something started to come through the blood. A small dome at first, it pushed through, the edge of the pool getting larger, until a face came through. A woman, facing the ceiling, being brought through a doorway to another world, another dimension. Will watched with his breath held.

It was working.

The woman rose from the doorway, the blood covering her as if she had just risen from a swimming pool, naked as the day she had been created. She was motionless in herself, with no movement other than the gentle float of her raising, until she stood in the centre of the pentagram, the blood flowing from her body. As it started to reveal her skin beneath, Will could see that she was beautiful. Her skin a translucent pink, completely hairless. Her eyes closed, her lips red with blood. She opened her eyes, drawn to the stare of Will, and smiled. "Why did you call me?" she asked, her voice silky, smooth, yet deep.

"Revenge," he said.

The woman nodded.

"I didn't expect … a woman," Will whispered.

She looked down at herself, her hand coming up to her breast and cupping it. "Hm," she grunted. Her hand dropped to crotch and she slipped her fingers in. "Mm." She removed them, bringing them to her mouth and tasted them. "You get what you are given, I suppose."

Will couldn't stop staring. He had no idea what she meant, but he would find out soon enough. For now, he was happy that he had raised a demon.

She ran her hands over her body, tenderly, feeling her way like she had never felt herself before. Like a child exploring with touch. She slipped her hands around behind her, looking like she was massaging the blood into her body.

Will could feel himself becoming aroused, but he didn't move. He was cross-legged on the floor. There was no way she could see. But she knew. She looked at him and smiled.

"It's been a long time since you felt that way, has it not?" She advanced on him, standing over him, the dribbles of blood still fleeing her body to the floor, and now she dripped onto Will's clothes. She bent down and put her forefinger under his chin and brought her face close to his. So close, he could smell her newness, somehow mixed with an age unbecoming of such beauty. "Do you want me?"

Will nodded slowly, unsure himself, confused at finding his cock hardening for the first time in months.

She smiled and took his hand. She pulled gently for him to get up from the floor, which he did without thinking. She led him through the flat, impossibly, straight to the bedroom. "How do you know …" he words drifted away. He felt stupid asking. He was being led to bed by a hairless, naked demon—one who he was expecting to be a man, or a male, or whatever. He guessed that he got whatever.

She shushed him. "I already know what *you* do," she said. "I know everything."

At the bed, she turned him to face her. Will leaned in to kiss her. They were so close, and she was only a slight smaller than he was. She pulled her head away. "No." She pulled his jeans from his cock and wrapped her hand around it, tugging on it gently. "You've been waiting."

"I couldn't," he replied.

Belphegor dropped to her knees slowly, immediately taking him in her mouth. She jerked his shaft with her hand, her lips around his head. She made approving sounds, while Will looked at the ceiling. His mind was awash with confusion. What was he doing? Here. Fucking a demon?

She stopped and stood, and Will brought his head down to look at her. She wiped the blood around her mouth with the back of hand, and then pushed him gently to the bed. He dropped to sitting, his face level with her breasts. "Suck them," she said.

Will looked at them. They hung firm, and he wanted to … but the blood.

"Suck them," she said again, this time firmer.

Will took her left nipple in his mouth and rolled his tongue around it. Perfect, except for the taste of blood. Then she squealed and pushed him back by the shoulders to lay on the bed. A wide, open-mouthed grin slipped across her face, and she straddled him. Sliding herself up his body, across his cock and then down, onto it.

She was wet. Soft, and smooth, but cold as ice on the inside. Will grunted in pleasure. She put her finger over his mouth. "Wait," she said, sliding up him and down again. He raised his hips to meet her thrust, but she pulled back, and when he dropped back to the bed, relaxing, she started to rocking against him again. She squeezed his cock with her cunt, like an icy fist.

Will was close.

As he started to ejaculate, she left him, let him shoot semen across his belly. "Hrrr," he grunted, an unsatisfactory orgasm slipping away too fast.

"Not this time," She said, getting up from the bed

and turning back to the door. "I'm hungry."

"Belphegor," Will said quietly, spent.

"Call me Belle," she said, leaving the room.

Will lay there. He was breathing shallow, but hard. He couldn't explain it. He looked down at his belly, down to his jeans hooked on his knees as they folded over the end of the bed. He sat up and reached down beside the bed, picking up a shirt and wiping the goo from his skin before it started to dry. He pulled the tee his was wearing down to cover it, and stood, his cock drooping. He dragged his jeans up and followed Belphegor—Belle—out. She was in the kitchen, the fridge door open in her hand, as she bent down and examined the contents. "Not much in, I've … been too busy to shop." He looked at her naked arse. "Sorry," he added.

She reached in and pulled an open pack of sausages from the shelf. She sniffed at them.

At first, Will thought it was to make sure they were still good. Did that matter to a demon? Who knew? "I can cook those for you," he said, turning to the cooker and twisting the knob on the gas.

Belle took one of the pork sausages (high meat content, too. Will was always particular about the quantity of meat in things that were made largely of intestines, testicles, and hoof), and raised it in a toast. "Chin-chin," she said, and bit into it.

Will recoiled at the sight, before realizing how silly he must look. He just performed a basic black magic ritual and raised a demon lord. Fucked it, too.

And he was worried about a sausage.

"Nice tats," she said, interrupting his thoughts.

He looked at his arm. The Enochian letters. "Yeah," he said.

"I do," she replied.

Will raised his eyebrows in question.

"I do know why they're there. So," she said, slipping the rest of the raw pork sausage into her mouth and chewing. "Are we going to do this, or what? I'm going to need clothes." She looked down at herself. "I haven't been to earth in a while, but I'm guessing a naked chick walking down the street might raise a few suspicions."

Will nodded, looking at her skin. "Of course," he said, shyly looking away.

"No need to be shy. We can fuck again when you're ready. I owe you. Would you like me to call you Master?"

The idea was appealing, but, "No," he said quickly.

Belle dropped her head to the side, shrugging. "Suit yourself. Will it is." She pointed out of the kitchen towards the bedroom. "I'll help myself then?"

Will nodded and she went to the bedroom. He could hear her rummaging.

CHAPTER 6

The most distracting thing, at least Will thought, was her lack of eyebrows.

Belle sat opposite him. They were outside the back of *The Anchor* pub in Northgate. It was a few miles from where Will lived, and they had taken the bus. Belle had raised a couple of looks from the oldies on the bus when they got on, but between the two of them, they were too scared, he expected, to stare for long. Belle had found a tee shirt that didn't have any sleeves, and was torn by design from the armpit to the seam at the waist. She didn't wear anything underneath it, revealing her breasts freely from most angles. She had taken a pair of jeans with the knees torn out, and hoisted them up with a studded belt. She didn't take a jacket saying she didn't feel the cold. Will was wearing the same clothes as last night, when they'd fucked, and it wasn't until they were trapped on the bus that he realized he stank of BO and cum. Between that and his ink, and that he had barely dragged a comb through his hair, it was no surprise that none of this people wanted to acknowledge them. He sipped his beer.

"So which one of them is supposed to be here?" Belle asked.

"I thought you could read my mind?" Will countered, genuinely interested.

"I can, but I don't. I found that knowing what everyone is thinking all the time and having their entire breadth of knowledge at my fingertips makes me a dull conversationalist."

"Huh. Anyway." He took another sip. "Del. He plays in the band." Will pointed to the posters that lined the fence looking out onto the dual carriageway.

"Dig Bicks," she said, reading the name of the band, slowly. "Nice. Clever."

Will got the sarcasm. "He never was subtle."

"So how do want to do this?" Belle watched the people as they passed. Now they were in the grounds of a pub in the early evening, her lack of hair and their general dress was raising less attention. She had a pint in front of her, but only at Will's insistence. He thought it would be weird if she didn't have the presence of a drink. Belle had asked the woman behind the bar if they had any raw meat, before Will intervened and laughed it off saying that was a Swedish cocktail. She'd gotten a pint of John Smith's in the end and was touching the glass occasionally, but hadn't picked it up. *I'll get you some sausages later,* he had assured her.

"I don't know." He replied. "What do you think? I thought you'd want to see what the guy looks like first."

She looked around. "Nah," she said. "Let's get it done tonight."

Will was slightly taken aback. "Okay."

"I could eviscerate him on the stage in front of

the crowd?" she mused.

"Er, no. That would be bad. I think it best if we keep it on the down low."

"Subtlety," she said. "Nice. Okay. How about I use my feminine charms to lure him somewhere private and then we get down to business?"

Will nodded. "That sounds better."

―

Belle stood to the side of the pubs tiny and ineffectual mosh pit. She had no interest in touching, or being touched, by the people that enjoyed this sort of music. Del was playing the bass in the band. He was slapping the guitar, and looked like he knew what he was doing, but Belle knew better. It was good showmanship, but the playing was substandard. The rest of the band bopped along, playing a number of mid-to-late nineties metal covers. Still, the crowd seemed to like it.

Belle just watched Del.

Del had noticed her. Of course he had noticed her. She watched him when he arrived, and she invaded his mind without his knowledge. She'd tenderly raped him. And now she stood there, long blonde hair. Eyebrows. The things that Del found attractive. The switch was easy. A cubicle. In as herself, out as Del's dream woman. Her shape was still the same, her facial features, but he liked blondes.

He'd winked at her.

And from there, she knew she had him.

As the set finished, Belle had prepared to talk to him, but then there were three damned encores. And the crowd loved it. Fucking substandard Megadeath. Murdering classics.

Finally, it finished.

Del seemed out of breath when she approached. Hopefully he wasn't one of those pretend musicians who just wanted to go home to bed alone after the gig. She walked straight up to him, gently pushing passed a couple of groupie whores, and almost fell into his arms. She rested her hand on his chest. "You were the best," she said.

Del laughed. She could feel him trying to decide which of the women in front of him was to his taste. The two whores were together. He could have them both, but he hadn't worked that out yet. He was slow. Neanderthal. And a little confused. She could feel him picturing himself with each of them. He was a filthy misogynist. Thinking about them like meat.

Meat.

Belle was hungry.

She leaned to his ear, whispering under the noise of the pub. "I'll let you do anything you want."

Del looked at her. *Anything?* he mouthed.

She nodded. Sealed.

CHAPTER 7

"Del and Belle." He giggled. Del had his arm over Belle's shoulder as the two of them walked from the gig towards the flat that Del had assured her was his alone. He'd even left his bass behind for the drummer to take, so he didn't need to wait. The promise of *anything* seemed to get him excited enough that not only did he leave there and then, but he didn't give the other two whores a look.

And Will walked behind them. Half a street back.

In the shadows.

They reached the front door of a block. It looked like shitty student accommodation. Del could see the look on her face, and said, "It's not as bad on the inside. Promise." He was naively sweet in his own rapist way. Belle turned to him and kissed him. It was gentle. It played into the way he was being so tender with her. She didn't want to scare him off. He responded, kissing her back, before opening the door and letting her go in first. She glanced over his shoulder as she ran her fingers gently under his chin, seeing Will waiting as agreed, far enough away to not arouse suspicion.

Not that Del was short on arousal at the moment.

She went into the hallway and leaned against the wall. It gave him a good look at her body. "Which way?" she asked. It was the basement. She already knew.

"Follow me," he said, brushing passed her *by accident*. He smiled awkwardly, and led her to the stairs at the back of the building and down one flight to a solitary door. He fumbled getting the key into lock.

He was all front. Inside the recesses of his mind Belphegor had slid around looking into all of the crevasses. She'd seen his wonts and desires. She'd seen his truth. Del wasn't the ladies man that he made out to be. He usually packed the shit up after the gig while Micky, the lead singer, got all the tail. Fuck, even the drummer got more action than this cunt. That's why he was so nervous. He rarely got this far. Not that women like Belle were what he really liked.

Not deep down.

He held the door open and Belle slipped by into the flat. It was dark. The hallway was narrow. Pokey. She waited for him to turn the light on, and then turned back to him, putting her hand behind his neck and drawing him in close to her face. "What do you want to do first?" she asked.

"Drink?"

Even Belphegor was surprised at the answer. Bless. He *was* nervous. "Why not?" She followed him through to the kitchen, where she waited for him to pour two drinks. He kept whiskey in the fridge. Weird. Even a demon could tell a lot about a man from his kitchen. The glance into the fridge showed only beer, fine, whiskey, still weird, and ready meals. The microwave was dirty. The worktops had food detritus over them. He didn't look after himself and he had no pride. She shrugged and took the cold whiskey from him, touching the glass to her lips, watching him over the rim of the glass. She took a sip, and asked him, "So what do you do for a living? Just the music?"

"Yeah, man." He relaxed into his drink. "I live for the music. You know, when I was growing up my old man used to hit me. I didn't do well in school. Fell in with a crowd. Don't do anything like that anymore."

Right.

"Music saved me. It gave me an outlet." He looked at the floor. "I don't know what I'd do without it."

Belphegor probed. It was a line. He was trying to get an emotional reaction from Belle. He was trying to manipulate her into bed. *This guy must have the IQ of a sprig of parsley.* She put her glass on the counter top—the whiskey was a shitty blend anyway—and walked over to him, putting her hand in the centre of his chest. "Poor you," she said. "What can I do to make it better?"

Del smiled at her, also resting his glass down. "Shall we go to the bedroom?" he asked, quietly.

Smooth.

She took his hand. "Lead the way."

Del drew her forward to the living area and through the far door into the bedroom. It was musty. Damp, even. There was black mold in one corner of the room, stark against the white walls. The mattress was on the floorboards, with no actual bed underneath, and there was a football team flag pinned, or possibly nailed, to the wall directly above the bed head.

Very tasteful.

"So what do you want? I said anything."

"Sit," he said, walking her to the bed and releasing her.

Belle tried to sit seductively, difficult when almost on the floor. "What?" she asked in a low voice.

Del waved for her to hush. He was still nervous. He went over to the wardrobe. Dark solid wood, out of place in such a minimalist room. He reached in and then stopped. He glanced back at her. "Anything?"

Belle nodded.

He pulled out a suit bag—a black garment carrier, zipped up, with a hanger out the top—and held it out to her without speaking. Belle took it. She played her part, looking at the bag with some sort of child-like wonder.

"It's never been worn," he blurted.

Belle nodded, and unzipped the carrier, looking inside. She nodded, and stood. "No problem," she said. "But how will I know you're not peaking, when I put it on?"

Del looked terrified rather than excited. She could see he was already hard in his jeans. "Wait," she said. "I know." She placed the carrier down with reverence, and took Del's hand. She led him gently to the mattress, and on to it, the two of them standing in the centre. She pushed him against the wall, covered by the flag and leaned against him. She took his wrists and raised them, hard against the wall, bringing them up to a crucifixion pose. She licked his lips and he muttered something biblical.

She straddled across him, against the wall, holding herself impossibly, like gravity was pulling her to the wall and not the floor.

Del felt it, he looked down at her. "Fucking hell," he said. "How the fuck are you doing that? Are you some sort of contortionist?"

"Something like that," Belle said. She leaned back, riding him cowgirl style against the wall, letting go of his left hand. He looked around wildly trying to work out how she was holding herself against the wall two feet from the mattress. She reached over to the corner of the flag and wrapped her fingers around the nail holding it up. What kind of cunt puts a flag up with four-inch nails? She laughed to herself. She pulled it out and the flag flopping down over his arm. He still looked confused. Poor boy. She raised the nail up and brought it down in a stabbing motion going through the palm of this right hand and impaling him to the wall.

Del screamed. "The fucking ..." And then he started to buck like a fucking bronco machine, stood against the wall, with a demon riding him.

"Yeeeeeeeeeeeeeee-*haw*," Belle screamed. She reached over and pulled the second nail from the flag with one hand and taking Del's flailing hand with the other. She gripped it, and he couldn't shake her. He looked around wildly trying to grasp what was happening. She was bending the laws of physics, and was strong as an ox. She pushed his left hand against the wall and impaled that one too.

Del made a succession of grunts and wails followed by the word cunt, several times. Belle got down from the wall and stood on the bed. She was close enough for him to reach her with his feet and he kicked her, but it was like kicking a concrete wall. She didn't move, or flinch, her femininity gone as she looked at him.

"What do you want?" he cried.

Belle smiled. She reached down and picked up a pair of stinking fucking boxers from the floor and stuffed them in Del's mouth as he fought to get free. Then she picked up the clothes carrier and left the bedroom closing the door.

Belle went to the sofa and dropped the carrier down, unzipping it and removing the contents. She smiled to herself. *Little man.* She pulled her tee over her head and her jeans off. Then she dressed in the little sailor outfit in the carrier. It was tight across her tits, and on her arse, but it worked well enough. She went to the door of the flat and out, up the stairs, and to the street. She went out and waved over Will.

As soon as he saw her, he broke into a run, across the street, grabbing her by the elbow and almost dragging her back into the house. "What the fuck do you think you're doing?" he said, slamming the front door. "You can't come outside dressed like that."

Belle raised an eyebrow. "Why?"

"People," he replied.

She shook her head. "You know I'm not this luscious creature, right? All delicate and feminine?"

Will shook his head. "Sorry," he said quietly. "You're right. Where is he?"

"In the bedroom, waiting for me to come back."

Will looked down at her clothes. "Yeah," he said. "About that. What the fuck …?" He let the question hang.

"Come on." She led him back down the stairs and into the flat. She took him to the living room and faced the door of the bedroom. "You're sure you want to do this?"

Will nodded, slowly. He was. He thought he was. "I'm leaving this in your hands," he said. "I want to watch him suffer."

"Suffer," she echoed. Next to the sofa, there was a dining chair. Weirdly, no dining table, just the chair. She picked it up, and took it with her into the bedroom. Will followed.

Belle placed the chair at the end of the bed opposite Del, still hanging from the wall. He'd stopped trying to free himself, the fight was gone. He watched her when she came in. His eyes drifted up and down her body clothed in the sailor suit. She faced him, asking, "Is this a slutty sailor suit, or is it supposed to be for a little boy?"

He shook his head.

Belle dropped her head to her shoulder in pity. "Oh, but you don't know. I can see everything inside that black, demented little head of yours. You are *so* confused in there."

Will came in, and Del's thrashing begun again. He pulled at the nails that held him up, blood letting from them, streaking down his hands to his wrists and dropping off, to the mattress at his feet.

Belle gestured for Will to sit in the chair, and he did as was expected of him. He faced Del while he took his time in recognizing him. The tats, the change in his hair. His mannerisms were all so different from six months ago. Del shook his head. Belle walked over to him and pulled the boxers from his mouth. He hungrily sucked the air in. "Will, man. What the fuck? What are you doing here?" He looked at Belle. "You've got help me. Get me down."

Will shook his head. "I don't think so." He smiled. "Belle here is … with me." She walked over to Will's side and he ran his hand over her half covered arse.

"What do you want?" Del blurted.

"What do you think?" Will's smile grew.

"Nah. I didn't do nothing to you. I never stuck you." He looked around. Having Will suddenly there seemed to clear his head, make him forget about the pain. He was looking for a way out. "I didn't do nothing later, either. I can help you. I know where Tim is. You'll never find him without me."

Will nodded. "Bargaining. What do you think?" He looked at Belle.

She shook her head. "I think we can find him without this one's help." She went over to Del and stood in front of him. She undid his belt, and popped the button on his jeans, pulling the two sides apart, lowering the zip. She crouched as she pulled his jeans down, and then did the same with his boxers.

He pulled on the nails, giving out a yell. Belle picked up his dirty boxers again and forced them into his mouth. She looked him up and down, crucified. She then returned to Will at the end of the bed and sat in his lap. She gyrated, sliding her arse over his cock, confined in his jeans. Will grunted. He couldn't see Del with Belle where she was, but he knew he was there, watching. He wasn't sure about Belle fucking him with an audience, though. She stood up and lifted the skirt of the suit, bending forward. Will couldn't help himself. He started to lap at her arsehole, rimming her with his tongue. She moaned out in pleasure. She rose a little, tearing the top of the costume over her head, still facing Del.

"Oh, God," she groaned. "Fucking yes." She brought her hand under the front of the skirt and started to finger fuck herself. "I'm gonna cum," she said. She looked up at Del. He was hard, trapped somewhere between pleasure and pain, his face contorted by the nails in his hands holding him up, but panting through the shorts in his mouth, aching to be touched. Belle stepped away from Will, and slid the skirt off. She stood there naked in front of the two men. She gave Will a quick look and winked at him, before turning her attention to Del. She crouched down in front of him and took his cock in her mouth. She felt him flex with pleasure, and then she bit down. Hard. Her teeth breaking the soft skin on the shaft, blood pouring from him, pushed by the pressure of his erection. It squirted over her face, into her mouth, down her chin, over her naked body. She laughed and fell back on the mattress, giggling, running her fingers through the blood, rubbing it into her tits, sliding her hands down, over her belly, to her slit, around, and in. Del didn't lose his hard-on at first, even with blood gushing from him. He was thrashing his head from side to side, as the blood pattered on the dirty sheets. As she laughed, he became flaccid.

Belle got to her knees and crawled naked to Will, taking his cock from his pants and sucking on it hungrily. He grunted in pleasure, his eyes not leaving Del. He watched him squirm as she pleasured him.

Belle stopped. She looked Will in the eyes. "Better," she said, pleased that he had lasted longer this time, and hadn't cum. "Hold on." She got up and padded from the room, leaving bloody footprints on the floorboards as she did. When she returned a couple of minutes later, Del's head was hung low, his skin pale. Blood pooled on the mattress, the caseless pillows saturated. He was still moving. She smiled at Will, who had his cock in his hand, stroking. "Good," she said. She had one of the knives from the kitchen in her hand. She went over to Del and raised his head with her hand. "Still with me?" she asked, before letting his head drop again. She turned her attention to Will, sitting there wanking. "It's a bit blunt." She turned back to Del and grabbed what was left of his mangled penis, taking the shaft and his balls in one hand and starting to slice the lot off with the knife. It brought Del back around and he started to thrash again, only this time he was weak. Barely trying. "It's more hacking than slicing," she said with brevity over Del's grunts of pain.

She got through the penis and it dropped from her grip, slopping onto the mattress. "Oops." She giggled, and finished hacking at his scrotum. Then she let that drop from her hand too, along with the knife. Del was unconscious, blood coming from his shattered groin, flesh and muscle, tendons, and veins hanging loose.

She turned back to Will, and crouched down in front of him again, taking his cock from his hand and into her mouth, pleasuring him until he finished, as he stared dead-eyed at Del's draining corpse.

Belle wiped the remnants of the spunk from her lips as she smiled staring at Will. He looked from the corpse to her and back again, letting out a short snort. "I'm hungry," she said.

Will winked at her. "You're going to have to give me a few minutes to recharge."

She slapped his legs. "Cheeky." She stood up and turned back to Del. "No, I'm really hungry."

"Ah."

She stepped onto the mattress, but stopped herself, before turning back to him. "You don't have to watch if you don't want to."

Will shrugged, but didn't move.

Belle licked her lips. She turned back to Del and dropped carefully to her knees. She picked his flaccid cock from the blood splattered mattress and sniffed at it.

"Ugh." Will stood. "I'll be, uh …" He gestured to the living room and followed the direction of his own motion.

Belle glanced back at him. "I won't be long."

He left the room.

Belle turned her attention back to Del's cock. She sniffed it again and tossed it to one side. It didn't smell … fresh. She clambered through the blood and testicles to stop, kneeling at Del's feet like she was worshipping him—or about to give him head. He would have liked the sentiment. She picked the knife back up from the mattress and stabbed it into his belly, just above his matted pubic hair, pulling it jaggedly across one side of his gut and then the other. She dropped the knife between his limp legs and reached into the stomach wound, rummaging around. She found a long, firm, tube and yanked it out. The large intestine. "Mm," she purred. "Sausage." She fed on the intestines from the body, and once she had enough to sate her, she picked the knife back up and hacked through the firm flesh of it. Lumps of undigested food slopped from the end, watery fluids hung viscous from the wound, and the smell of fresh shit rose from the now loose tube. "Oh," she said, waving her hand in front of her nose. "Dear Lordy." She looked up at Del's face. "You probably weren't well, anyway." She smiled and gnawed on the intestine in her hand, tearing the flesh from it with her teeth.

"Yummy."

CHAPTER 8

Belle sat with her feet dangling off the side of Will's bed. "'S next?" she asked. She was twiddling with her hair.

"Jason," he said. "I want Tim last." He shot her a glance as he pulled his shorts back up. "When are you going to get rid of that?" He nodded at her hair.

She spread her legs and slapped the hair between her legs. "Aw. You no likey?" She giggled. "Spoil sport." She pouted.

Will flashed her a quick smile. "You know me."

Belle shuffled off the bed. "Bacon it is." She stood and left.

Will watched her go. His life was getting stranger and stranger. Not only had he started to behave more like a normal human being again—for the first time in months—since her arrival less than a week ago, but she'd fallen into the role of his girlfriend with some ease. He stood and pulled a shirt over his head without unbuttoning it. And the things they were doing … he shrugged it from his thoughts. There was no sense in dwelling on that. She was what she was. Maybe after they had finished doing this then she would stay? Who knew?

Will followed the smell of bacon out into the hallway and to the kitchen. Belle stood naked in front of the frying pan. "You wanna watch yourself," he said. "You'll get burned."

"Already have been," she said. She poured the bacon from the pan onto a plate and turned to Will passing it to him. "So what's the plan?"

Will had noticed that she had no interest in either food, nor drink. He also noticed that the hair between her legs was gone.

She saw him looking and giggled, turning away.

Will picked up a piece of the fried meat and chewed on it, thinking. "We should be able to pick up Jason somewhere around here. I've spoken to some people who have seen him around."

Belle nodded. "Suffering?"

"Very much so."

"Do you want to watch again?"

Will nodded, his face flushing red.

"Tonight."

"That soon?"

Belle smiled. "No time like the present, right?" She slipped passed him ensuring that she pushed her body against his. Will lifted the plate over her head as she left, before stuffing another piece of bacon into his mouth.

———

"Here."

The two of them stood outside The George. "You're sure," said Belle. She rested her hand on his arm. "You haven't been here since that day."

Will looked at her. It still bothered him that she sometimes knew things that she shouldn't. She'd said that she didn't mean to, but when he had intense thoughts about something they bled out into her mind. She could hear them, without listening. It was a beautiful way for her to say that she could feel his lingering pain. At least, *he* thought so. "I know," he said, quietly. "It's fine." A lie. He knew it. He knew that she knew it. He wasn't looking forward to this

"Who's Cherry?" Belle asked.

Damn. "No one," he lied again.

Belle frowned, but took Will's arm regardless and the two of them went in the pub. It was evening, and the place was busier than he remembered. He always remembered it as empty, Cherry behind the bar. It was how he wanted to remember it. The two of them stood by the door, while Belle waited for Will to become comfortable enough to enter properly. It was busy enough that he couldn't see behind the bar. People in the way. He couldn't see the faces of everyone in the place. There was probably more in the poolroom around the back. He led Belle to the edge of the bar where there was a single empty stool. He slapped it, letting Belle take the seat. She smiled at him like a girlfriend would, slipping up onto the stool and sliding around to face the bar, her man on her shoulder. Will took a twenty out his wallet and held it, resting his hand on the bar top, note up.

A young man came over quickly. "What'll it be?" He looked at Belle with some unconscious desire.

Tonight she had cropped hair on one side of her head, long on the other. Eyebrows. There was a tattoo of a dragon crawling around her neck, disappearing into the collar of her torn tee. Will was used to people looking at her like that. She seemed to exude some sort of pheromone that effected just about everyone. He had never asked her about it, but he knew it was there. Even when she looked … different … people still seemed to want her.

"Pint of Snakebite and Black," Belle answered, looking into his eyes. He probably thought she was flirting. She wasn't. She was looking into his soul, his heart.

He snapped out of it, remembering that he worked there, his eyes flicking to Will, and his eyebrows raising.

"Same," Will replied to the unspoken question.

The barman went off to prep the drinks and the two of them stayed in silence. Belle was staring at the bottles behind the bar, but Will thought she was probably scanning the room with her mind, for her own edification. He was also looking around. He was trying to see if he knew anyone in here. There were a couple of guys from the site in the corner. He'd lost his appenticeship soon after Tim had … Will brushed away the memory under a rug in his head. The two of them hadn't seen him and he certainly didn't want to open a conversation with them. There was an empty table near the door to the poolroom. He tapped Belle on the shoulder and nodded for her to go over and sit. He'd bring the drinks over.

As the two of them sat there, they both watched people come and go. Belle knew exactly who she was looking for, even though she had never seen him before. Will had just returned with another two beers. He'd drunk the first two. "Nothing." He slurred a little when he spoke.

Belle looked at him, but didn't speak.

"What's the point?" He started to neck the next pint.

"Watch that shit," she said. "It'll have you off your feet."

Will looked at her over the glass as he tipped it. His eyebrows spoke for his lips.

Belle shook her head. As she watched, the door to the pub opened. Two people came in. A man and a woman. She nudged Will and nodded to the two of them as they crossed to the bar, oblivious to their presence.

Will looked up, and he watched Jason as he walked, holding hands with some girl.

"Fucker," he said. Will stood up, taking one of the empty glasses. "Another?" he asked, heading straight to the bar without waiting for an answer. Belle watched him. He was going to do something stupid.

Will walked straight to the bar and pushed his way in between Jason and whatever poor schmuck was sitting on the next stool. He picked up schmuck's beer glass, which was still full, and swung it without word into the face of the girl that was with Jason, just behind his shoulder. Had the glass not shattered, it would have only broken her nose. But it did.

Beer went everywhere.

The glass broke in Will's hand cutting into the flesh made soft by not working on the site for so many months. He dropped what was left of the glass, shards sticking out of him, to the floor. The girl screamed, and the commotion started.

Belle was watching from the table, and simply said, "Fuck."

Jason looked at Will, there was a second of blankness, no recollection, no memory of the violence. The shanking. The rape. Then Will saw the cogs turn far enough that he recognized him through the haircut and the tats, a slow, Neanderthal recognition, something that suddenly seemed to make Jason scared. Scared shitless. Then he realized what had happened and he screamed, "*Trish.*"

Will grinned at him, and then shouldered his whole weight onto Jason, pushing him from the barstool to the floor of the pub. Will straddled him like Belle would do to him when she was fucking him. Jason had the wind knocked out of him, and although a number of people seemed to suddenly be moving about and screaming, no one was actually *doing anything*. At least, not to Will. He raised his right hand, the one without the broken glass sticking out of it, and jabbed it into Jason's face. His head rocked back hard onto the tile floor of the pub, making a pocking sound as it bounced off the floor. Will's first punch split his lip, and the blood let hard and fast, onto Jason's chin, up his nose, and onto Will's knuckles. Then he punched him again. He caught his cheek. Jason's head bounced off the floor again. This time his face started to swell around one eye, turning green, the eyelid closing down. Jason's other eye lolled around in the socket, unable to focus on what was going on. Jason raised his hand for a third punch, but someone locked their arm around his and started to pull him away. "No, you cunts," he shouted, trying to get back to his target. "Fuck him." They pulled Will away, and across the floor of the pub. Two of them. One holding each arm. "You rapist fuckers," he shouted at them, no longer in the moment, but caught somewhere in the past.

"Fucking, Jesus Christ." Belle stood up and clicked her fingers.

The man holding Will's good arm back, suddenly released him, bringing both his hands to his head, cradling his ears. He looked like he was being deafened by something no one else could hear.

Will took the opportunity to swing his now free hand and strike whoever had a hold of his other arm. The guy let go, falling away. Will ran forward and knocked the barman who was leaning over Jason to the side. He stomped Jason's face, breaking his nose open, blood slooped onto the floor, and Jason screamed blue fucking murder.

Will laughed.

Belle appeared at his side. "What the fuck do you think you're doing?"

Will stomped on him again. This time his head jerked to the side and lay motionless. He stopped and looked around the pub. No one was moving. They were all motionless in whatever they were doing. He looked at someone who was standing on the sidelines, watching, their cider spilling over the side of the glass, hung in midair. He stopped, panting. "What the fuck?"

"This wasn't the plan," she said. "You're drunk."

He turned on her. "What are you, my mum? Did you stop time? I didn't know you could do that."

Belle raised her hand again, fingers together ready to click. "Do you want me to restart all this? Without me, you'll have no more revenge."

Will hesitated. He looked around at the people. Most of them seemed to be gunning for him. He looked at Jason, bloodied on the floor and pointed at him. "That's not enough. I want him to suffer."

Belle stepped up next him. "And what about her?"

Trish was laying on her back, her eyes puffed out and swollen, her nose crook. There were shards of glass sticking out of her eyelids, piercing through into her eyes. Blood coming from her mouth.

Will shrugged.

"That's all you've got?" Belle asked.

"I thought you were supposed to be the demon here. Where are your balls?"

Belle sighed. "Oh, for fuck's sake," she said, shaking her head. "Yes, Master."

Sarcasm.

CHAPTER 9

"So." Will let the word hang in the air. They were back at his flat. Standing in the kitchen. He was staring at Belle, his eyebrows raised, waiting for an explanation. First they were in the pub. Now they were here. "What's this fucking game?"

Belle raised her hand to hush him. "I didn't sign up for this."

"You're a fucking demon. I raised you to help me feel …" *What? Better about himself?* "… something."

"And I thought this would be fun." She shrugged. "I brought you back here to stop you from doing something stupid. Something else … stupid."

"And about that. When were you going to tell me that you could flit about the earth like a shadow?"

"You never asked."

"We took the bus to Ashbury, to get Del," he said, exasperated.

Belle smiled at him. "Getting to know you?"

Will turned away. "You're fucking useless."

Belle sighed. *Oh, the drama.* "Okay," she said. "I'll be straight up with you. I don't know what books you've been reading, or what TV shows you think have given you some deep insight as to what power you think you have over me, or what you think I'm doing here, but I'm here because I chose to be here, bucko." She grabbed his shoulder and turned him around, manhandling him with the fortitude of a wrestler. "I'm not here to do your bidding. I chose to come. And you want to know why?" Will looked away and she slapped him like his mum. He looked back. "Those three—those three fuckers who wrecked you. The one's who broke you. Took the innocence from you. Them? I had them. They were all coming to Hell regardless. But you—you were all sweetness and light. So I thought I could nudge you along the way too."

"You want my soul?"

"I've got your soul now. What did you think after we cut some dude's cock and balls off, and fucked over it? Saint Peter's gonna strike it off, because Delly-Welly was mean to me? *We cut his cock off and he bled to death.*"

Will let his head hang down. "You used me."

"Jesus on a stick," she said. "So fucking what?"

Will barged passed her out of the room and Belle followed him. He went into the bedroom and slumped on the bed, his head in his hands. She stood at the door and waited for him to do whatever. Lose his shit, probably.

"And there's nothing I can do about it?"

"Almost certainly, but I'm hardly going to tell you what, now, am I?"

He looked at her, tears in his eyes. "I guess."

"So, now we've got that out of the way, how

about we finish what we started? Would that make you feel better? I mean, I'm under no obligation, of course. But, heck, I'm here. May as well have some more fun."

Will nodded, slowly. "When will you take my soul?" he asked, quietly.

"When you die, whenever that is. Same as everyone else. Blow job?"

CHAPTER 10

Belle stood at Will's side as they watched Jason from a distance. "Grab and go?" he offered her a crisp.

"Seems a bit simple." Belle stuck her hand in the bag and pulled out a handful of bits from the bottom. "Worcester Sauce flavoured crisps are weird."

"They are." Will tipped the bag into his mouth, taking the last of them. He had decided not to worry about the whole soul thing for now. As Belle has said, *what was he going to do about it?* "Where *is* he going?"

Belle pointed out to the beach huts under the lip of the cliff. "What about those?"

Will shook his head. "Doesn't seem much like a beach hut kind of guy, does he?"

Belle shook her head. The two of them had followed Jason as he left his mum's house, heading towards the beach. Will had forbidden them from doing anything at the house. He didn't think it was fair on his mum. Bless. Jason had hooked around the hospital grounds on the way, and Will thought he was going to see Trish—blinded permanently by the *incident*—but he had gone on by. Probably didn't want to fuck her now she was a cripple. And now he was down on the beach and wandering across the wet sand, cutting the corner off the prom.

The cold weather precluded there being a lot of people on the beach. It was empty.

The two of them stuck to the prom as Del walked over the sand, he was heading for the spit that led to the next bay, only accessible while the tide was out.

Will and Belle reached the end of the prom, blocked by fallen cliff face, and waited there, sharing a second bag of crisps—full English breakfast flavour—while he ambled along slowly.

"These taste like farts," said Belle.

"It's the egg."

He disappeared around the rock formation and out of sight.

"Where the fuck is he going?"

"Let's find out." Belle jumped down from the prom and started to hurry across the sand, followed by Will. They only had a few minutes before the tide was going to start to come back in.

At the spit, they watched. Jason followed the cliffs back toward the beach carefully, before disappearing into the rocks.

"He's gone in a fucking cave," Will said.

"Interestinger and interestinger," Belle replied.

They waited. Only a couple of minutes later, Jason reappeared, leaving in the same direction he came, heading straight back towards them. Will turned and hurried around the corner out of sight, with Belle shortly behind him. "Wait," he said. He regarded the beach. There was no one. Apart from the wind, there wasn't even sound. "Here," he said.

"What? I thought you liked it messy."

"Let's just get rid of Jason and then we can deal with Tim. I want Tim to suffer unimaginably."

"You're the boss."

Will and Belle went over the rock pools close to the cliff and climbed a few feet up. It was enough to ensure that when Jason came around the corner, assuming he was going to go the same way that he came, he wouldn't immediately see them and bolt. He didn't disappoint. He came around the corner and walked straight across the sand away from the cliff. Will jumped down, unheard behind him, and ran over to him pushing him from his feet.

Jason fell onto the soft sand and rolled onto his back. "What the fu—"

He immediately recognized Will and started to push himself away on his back, trying to create distance. His nose was still mashed in from the pub fight and dark purple bruising covered the left of his face.

"Hush, little man." Will smiled at him. "First off," he called above the noise of the surf, getting closer, "what *are* you doing out here?"

Jason plunged his hands into the pocket of his jacket and pulled out a bag. "For Tim, that's all." He tossed the bag to Will's feet. "Keep it."

Belle had joined him and she bent down and picked the bag up. "Heroin," she said.

Will shot a glance with a raised eyebrow.

"I can tell by looking." She grinned. "It's fun finding things out instead of just looking into people's minds and knowing them, isn't it?"

Will stepped towards Jason. "And where might we find Tim?"

Jason shook his head. "No fucking way. He'll kill me."

"Aaaaannnddd, we won't?"

Jason looked around wildly.

"Seriously. Where is Tim?"

Jason looked longingly at the prom, the cliffs in the distance. "You can find him at Carter's, the old youth club. He's kipping in the basement. Got chucked out of his missus place for hitting her, and his old man won't take him back because of that shit." He waved at Belle. "I've been volunteering there for a while. I let him sleep down there."

"Very Samaratinus of you."

"Samaratinus?" Belle whispered.

Will shrugged. "Keys," he gestured for Jason to throw them.

Jason rummaged around in his jeans pocket and pulled a small bunch of keys out, chucking them over to Will. He looked at Belle. "You were there, I remember you."

Belle nodded, pocketing the Heroin baggie. "Yep." She leaned into Will's shoulder. "What do you want?"

"Fuck him," Will replied, loudly enough that Jason could hear.

"Will do." She took a stride towards Jason, before quickly turning back to Will. "See what I did?" She held her mouth gaping open. "*Will* do? Hah!" She turned away and advanced on Jason.

If Jason had been more aware of who Belle was and made more of an effort to get away, he probably had time to get to his feet and run. It wouldn't have made a difference, but it would have given him something in hindsight to think about. Not that there was much time left for him to *hindsight*.

Belle reached down, with Jason still on his elbows, laying on the sand, the water just creeping around him now, and grabbed him by the jeans. She picked him up like he was the weight of a watermelon, and twirled him around to his knees, resting him on all fours, like a baby. She tore his jeans off, ripping them open. He screamed as the denim ripped and pulled at his skin. She pulled his pants down. He'd already shit himself. "You really are a baby," she said. She pulled her fist back like she was in a boxing ring, and slammed it into his arsehole.

Jason let out a wail that cut off quickly.

"I'm in the bowel," she said. "Warm." Belle moved her hand deeper into him, wearing him like a puppet, and Jason wailed again. "Colon." Then Jason started screaming. She turned and looked at Will. "I'm waving at you." She laughed, and pulled her hand out roughly. It was covered in blood mixed with shit from the tips of her fingers to near the elbow. "Now I know what a vet feels like." Jason's arse gaped open and blood pumped from it like the tap had been opened on a caravan's sewage pipe. He cried out in pain, facing the sand, unable to move. She wrinkled her nose and smiled at Will.

Will nodded. "Very inventive, but do shut him up."

She saluted with her blood hand, leaving a small imprint on her forehead. She turned and pushed his face down into the sand, below the level of the pooling water. He flapped his arms briefly, before slumping forward. She lay him out flat as the water lapped against him, washing her hand and arm in the water. "Wanna fuck?" she asked Will as she straightened.

He looked around. "Maybe later," he said.

CHAPTER 11

Carter's Youth Club was in the shit end of the shit part of the town. There was an Aldi opposite it. Everyone in the surrounding area was unemployed. There was a nice curry shop. Only legend told of what the building was before it was a youth club. It was a youth club when Will was little. His mum had taken him to a judo class there when he was about eight and had nearly gotten his nose broken.

These days it was a refuge for troubled teens. At least, that was what it claimed to be. Sure, at some point in the past it was run by good people trying to make a difference, but these days it was run by 'Jasons', letting their mates stay there for free, probably having parties in the unused spaces. Fucking.

"What is it?" Belle asked as the two of them stood in Aldi's car park staring at the building.

"Like you don't know." He dismissed her comment and crossed the street to the building. It was still early. The place wouldn't open for the kids until lunchtime. Places like this needed to be open all the time. Not just when they felt like it. Will went to the front door and started trying keys.

"What if it's alarmed?" Belle asked.

"Nah. Not with Tim in here." She nodded, as Will found the right key and the door popped open. "Et, voila."

"Great."

Will looked at her. "Once this is over, what happens to you?"

"I don't know," she mumbled. "Whatever I feel like."

"Hm." Will opened the door quietly and stepped in. "No alarm," he said. The two of them entered and he closed the door behind them, locking it.

Echoing around the building, they could hear a clunk ... clunk. Metal. Heavy.

Will pointed across the entrance hall and over to the hallway that led deeper into the building. He hadn't been in here since he was eight. He was just following the sound.

Clunk.

Will stopped at the corner, waving Belle to wait behind him. She came up next to him slapping his hand down like a naughty schoolboy. "*Behave*," she scolded. She looked around the corner with him. It was an open floor, wide like a school assembly hall. None of the standard gym equipment though. There was a desk to the left with paperwork on it. Leaflets, signing in sheets and such, sat in a mess. Over the other side of the room was a semi-circle of sofa's, empty. A TV in the corner. It looked like a doss-hole. And the whole place smelt a little of sweat. But that could be Tim.

Clunk.

Belle walked around Will and the corner and

across the room towards the door on the far side. It was where the sound was coming from. She opened the door a crack and looked through. From behind her, Will could see it was shadowed in darkness. "Stairs," she whispered, pulling the door open. They led downwards.

Will nodded her forward. If she wanted to be in the lead, then so be it. Belle started down in silence. She could move with the grace and speed of a deer when she wanted to. Will wasn't so lucky. He seemed to find every creaking floorboard as he went down behind her, and for every one, she shot him a disapproving look. At the bottom of the stairs was a fire door. The noise came again, muffled from behind the door. Belle rested her hand on the door and pushed it open a little. The light came from behind. She opened the door far enough to get her head around it, and then pushed it properly open, finding the room beyond empty.

Will followed her in. A locker room. There was a camp bed in the corner. A sheet strewn across it. It must have been where Tim had been sleeping. The room was walled with lockers and two long benches rode the centre of the room. The clunk came again, from beyond the double doors on the other side of the room. Belle went over and looked carefully through the window in the door. She waved Will over with a grin.

He joined her and looked through. A gym.

"Interesting," she whispered. "Looks like we can have fun in there."

Tim was in the middle of the room, equipment set up all around him. He was lifting weights on a bench, laying down, pushing the bar straight up and down above his chest. It didn't look like he had that much weight on it. Will didn't know much about gyms, but he was fairly sure that you weren't supposed to lift on your own.

It was very dangerous.

He raised a smile. "Shall we?" The two of them pushed the doors open together, and walked in, purposefully across the room to Tim, not giving him a chance to prepare himself for anything. By the time he'd managed to spurt "What the fuck," and put the weights back on the bell rest, the two of them were over him.

He went to sit up and Belle pushed her hand down on his chest, her immense strength holding him in place. He looked up Belle first examining her, trying to work out what she wanted, if he knew her, perhaps? Then he looked at Will, doing the same. He was looking at them upside down, so it took a few minutes of them staring at each other in silence, until the penny seemed to drop for Tim.

"Fucking William," he said. "Long time no see." He grinned at Will. Shit eating fucker. "What can I do for you, and this, ravishing may I say, young lady."

Will squinted at him.

"Strong, isn't she?" Tim teased.

"Get him up," Will said.

Belle looked at Will, "Up?"

"Not like that."

She giggled, and pulled Tim to his feet. He was shirtless. Sweating. He was wearing a pair of exercise shorts and a pair of running shoes. Nothing else. Will looked at him as Tim regarded him up and down, almost daring him to do whatever he was going to do.

"Now what, big boy?" he asked.

Will could see his eyes flicking around the room. He was looking for a way out. Looking for a weapon, perhaps. "I think we should shut you up, first."

Belle walked him over to the chest press machine and forced him to sit, while Will picked up a couple of skipping ropes. They tied his wrists to the handles of the machine, leaving him sitting there looking at them. He tried to move his arms, test the weight of the machine. He could bring his arms together a little, but then he was spent, dropping the weight's back down. "It's because I've been lifting," he said.

Belle raised one side of her mouth. "Like we give a shit." She turned to Will who was walking the room. "Something about shutting him up?"

"Yes." Will hefted a dumbbell. He felt the weight of it. He held it in his hand as he jabbed at the air.

"Jokes over," Tim said quietly. He was scared.

"Joke was over a long time ago," Will replied, walking back over to him, carrying the bell. He raised it up and slugged it into his mouth. Normally a stupid place to plant a punch—full of teeth. The cast iron bell snapped his neck back into the cushion of the high backed seat of the machine. Tim grunted at first, bringing his head back upright before staring blearily at Will. He opened his mouth, full of blood, leaving it to drain down his chin and onto his chest. Bits of broken tooth crept along in the river of blood, with Tim trying to spit it out, spittle mixed with blood clinging onto his lips like cheese pulling from a pizza. He said something, but Will couldn't quite make it out. Cunt, perhaps?

"Now that," Belle pointed at Tim's mashed lower face, "is a turn on. What do you think lover?"

"Later," Will replied. There was an anger growing inside him, much like the one in the pub, but this time he wanted to control it, not the other way around. He dropped the dumbbell and looked around the room for something else. He was aware that Tim was pulling against the ropes, but he didn't care. Belle would make sure he stayed there.

Will went out across the gym floor and stuck his head through one of the other doors. "Shower," he said to no one. Across to the next. He went in. A small kitchen. Sink. Fridge. Not much. He opened the drawers. Basic cutlery. Butter knives, that sort of thing. What could be expected in a place like this though, with the sort of people you might get down here? He picked up the tin opener and prodded it into the middle of his palm. Blunt. He tossed it back in the drawer. Opened the fridge and crouched. Milk bottles. He took one, smelt the milk—off—and set it on the draining board. The only other thing in the fridge was some bananas. "Right." He stood back up and took the bottle back into the gym where Tim was sitting, blood still weeping from his mouth, but now his lips were badly swollen. He put the bottle on the bench across from Tim and continued over to the last door. It was locked. He cupped his hands together and looked through the window that was veined with wires. "Ah," he said. He pulled Jason's set of keys from his pockets and started trying them one at a time in the lock. He could hear Tim thrashing. Panic.

He found the right key and opened the door. It was a caretakers closet, with a set of metal shelves. Will took the toolbox from the second shelf and carried it across to the bench where the milk bottle was. He knocked the bottle off with the toolbox, the rancid milk glooped onto the floor like yogurt.

"Fucking hell," Belle said, holding her nose.

Will squinted at her. "You're a demon. Grow up."

Tim looked at Belle and Will couldn't make up his mind if he was confused or terrified.

Will opened the tools and took them from the box, laying them out next to the box for Tim to see. Hammer. Nice. Screwdriver set. Useful. Pliers. Hm. He held the pliers, clicking them open and shut a few times. Tim kicked out.

Will took the pliers over to the chest press machine and clicked the pliers in front of Tim's face, before clasping them onto the overgrown, dirty nail of his left thumb. Then he pulled. The nail snapped before he'd gotten it from the skin, splitting and digging into Tim's flesh. Tim wailed out in pain, trying to withdraw his hand, but unable to. Will laughed. He moved to the forefinger next and tried again. This one came away from the nailbed with ease, only splitting the skin by the knuckle as it pulled away from the quick. Tim screamed again, with Will nodding along like it was the beat of a metal song. Then he took the next, another, and the last, from the pinky. With each nail, there was the initial struggle, then the pop of the release, in time with the scream of Tim. After each came away, Will dropped it to the floor.

Then he picked up the hammer.

Will's left hand was bloody, but largely undamaged. Will held it by the wrist and brought the hammer up over his head, bringing it down hard onto Tim's fingers. Tim wailed more and Will looked at Belle. "Too much?" he asked.

"You do you." She shrugged. She looked bored, leaning against an exercise bike.

So he brought it up again and down. The centre of the back of Tim's hand this time. The bone gave, splintering under the skin, poking shards through the surface. Will huffed as the excitement, the adrenaline, grabbed him and shook him. He had waited for so long.

He looked at Tim, screaming, but he couldn't hear it. He wasn't in the same place. He was somewhere else. Enjoying the moment. He dropped the hammer into Tim's lap and went and got a screwdriver. It was a foot long. He pressed it into the soft area of the shoulder just below the ball joint. It didn't slip in as easy as he had expected, so he took his other hand and pushed his palm against the screwdrivers handle and drove it harder. Once the shaft of it was in, it became easier, sliding up to the handle, passing through Tim and out the other side. He thrashed, but his head started to loll. Will pulled the screwdriver out and slapped him.

"Too much pain," Belle said. "He's slipping out of consciousness."

"Fucker," Will screamed into his face. "You stay awake for me."

The scream seemed to bring Tim back. At least to a state of semi-consciousness. Will untied his hands and took his feet, pulling him from the machine onto the floor, flat. Tim flopped about trying to fight back, to get up, but he flooped like a drowning fish. Will dropped down, straddling him across the chest. "You keep your eyes open." Will raised the hammer over his head, Tim watching him.

He slammed the hammer into the top of his head, popping it like a watermelon. The hammer stayed there, wedged in, Tim staring glazed at Will. He was still breathing, methodically, but his fight was gone. It was like his mind had left his body behind and gone shopping. Will wriggled the hammer back and forth to release it and Tim twitched a little. Once out, Will raised it up and hit Tim again. His brains, punctured and mashed dribbled from the top of his head like custard. Thick, and yellow. Brain fluid slid across the floor, pooling with blood. Will let go of the hammer.

Belle walked over, standing in Tim's brain matter, her feet either side of his head, leaving Will's head level with her hips. "Better?" she asked.

Will huffed, nodding, trying to get air into his lungs. He felt a little light headed.

Belle crouched, queening over Tim's lifeless messed up head.

Will could see up her skirt. She wasn't wearing any knickers. "Wanna fuck?" she asked.

He nodded, and she stood, taking his shoulders and guiding him to the floor. He lay in Tim's pooling blood and she unbuttoned his fly, opened his jeans and roughly pulled them from him. She lifted her tee over her head revealing her naked body beneath. Belle pulled the short skirt up over her hips and sat down on Will's cock as it flexed, aching for her. She rode him slowly at first, as he lay there watching her rock back and forth. She let her hands wander, rolling over Tim's corpse. She slid her fingers into his head, bringing them out covering in brain and transparent fluid, mixed with blood and shards of skull. She squished the bits between her fingers, dropping them onto Will's chest and she rode harder. She cupped her breast with her bloody hand, squeezing his cock with her cunt. She started grunting, triggering something in Will. He bucked, cumming hard inside her.

As his back relaxed, and his arch lowered, she slipped from him. "So it is done," she said.

Will lay on the floor, spent. He wiped the bits of Tim from his chest and flicked them across the floor. "Yeah."

Belle got to her feet, pulling her skirt down. She

picked up her tee. "Kebab?" she asked.

CHAPTER 12

Belle sat on the edge of the bed. The sun had just peeked in through the bedroom window and Will was still asleep, his torso half out from under the covers, his feet sticking out the end. "So," she wiggled his toes. "Do you want some breakfast?"

Will wrenched himself up onto an elbow. "Hm?"

"Sleep well?"

"Hm."

"Morning person, much." She smiled and stood, pulling the shirt he was wearing last night on over her naked body.

"What's happening today?" Will slung his feet out from the bed and to the carpet. He needed to vacuum. "I need some coffee."

"What do you mean, *what's happening today?*" She padded barefoot from the room.

Will stretched his arms above his head and rubbed his balled fists into his eye sockets. They'd fucked several times last night in celebration of the completion of the job. He felt like a weight was lifted. Not as high as he had hoped that it would have been, but it was gone from across his shoulders. He stood and poked around in the pile of laundry, pulling a pair of shorts from it. He held them up. At least they were blood less. There was a stain just to the side of the fly by that was probably ice-cream. Probably. He sniffed them, and satisfied he pulled them on, following her to the kitchen and the sound of the kettle rumbling.

Will slumped down on one of the chairs at the small table in the corner of the kitchen and waited for Belle to make the coffee, which she did in silence. She slid his mug in front of him and slipped into the chair opposite. He sipped the warm liquid and glanced at her, a small frown on his face.

"What?" she asked.

"I was just wondering what your plans are for today."

They fell into an uncomfortable silence, while Belle just stared at him. She finally responded. "Are you trying to get rid of me?"

"No." Will hurriedly shook his head. "No, not at all. I … love having you here. I just thought …" his voice trailed off.

"Thought I would, what, piss off back to wherever I came from? Is that it?"

Will shrugged. "I wouldn't have put it so bluntly but yes. I assumed that once I had achieved my goal—and having found out that you had some underhanded *other* reason to be here which has already been satisfied—that you would *piss off back to wherever you came from*."

Belle smiled. "But I kinda like it here."

"Hm," Will grunted. He focused back on his coffee. He didn't want to piss her off. But equally he wasn't looking at having a forever after companion.

Even if the sex was good.

"Amazing," she said, interrupting his thoughts.

"What?"

"The sex is amazing. At least from your point of view." She tapped her temple and smiled. "Don't forget I know what's going on up there, you know."

"Get out of my *head*." Will slammed the coffee mug down on the table too hard and some gushed over the side, spilling onto the shit plastic table. "And what do you mean, *from my point of view?*"

Belle smiled petulantly at him. "I've had better."

The weight from Will's shoulders returned and his muscled knotted. "Well if that's what you think, you can fuck right off."

"Right," she replied. She picked his coffee mug from the table and walked over to the sink, pouring it in.

"What the f—" He stopped himself. He probably deserved that. "Sorry," he mumbled. "You can stay I suppose, I just—"

"No," she interrupted him. "No. Quite. I should go. Go about my infernal business. It's me, it's not you. I thought we had something. I *thought* you wanted me to hang around."

"Well you do apparently have possession of my eternal soul now. We will be together forever, I assume."

"You assume incorrectly. Once you get down

there it won't all be weird-ass fucking, and brain lube, you know. Yes, I said it. What you asked me to do last night was weird. Anyway. I'll be off then."

"Where?" Will asked. Suddenly the realization that he was going to be alone for the first time in a few weeks struck him. He didn't want to be alone. Then he thought of Cherry. Maybe she was still single? *Maybe she was single before? You never asked.* He should see what she was up to. Ask her out. Yes. That was a great idea. He was more practiced in bed now. He was more … together than he was before.

Belle snapped her fingers under his nose. "You drifted off there, snowflake."

"Hm?" He looked her in the eyes. "Yeah. So, you're off."

She planted her hands on the table and pushed herself to standing. "I am."

He looked her down. "You might want to put on some knickers. Or trousers. Something?"

She snorted at him and clicked her fingers again.

Then she was gone.

Will stared at the space where she just was. He'd never witnessed something just vaporize before. It was … cool. Anyway. She'd disappeared back to wherever, and he wasn't about to worry about his immortal soul for now. He felt good. Great, in fact.

This was shaping up to be the best decision of his life.

CHAPTER 13

Will stood in front of the mirror on the wardrobe door. It was cracked but it would do. He was trying to straighten his cuffs. The shirt was brand new. It still had the creases in it from the packet and they didn't sit right on his arms. He should have just sucked it up and ironed one he already had, but *fuck that noise.* He just wanted to look his best, and cover the majority of his ink. She'd see the letters, the words, and ask questions. He also wanted to look presentable. After what had happened in the George last week he wasn't even sure if he should go.

But he hadn't had any repercussions from the police.

Which in retrospect, was weird. Will stared at himself in the mirror. Had nobody grassed him up? That seemed unlikely. Improbable. Even James hadn't said anything? Trish? He buttoned the shirt up to the collar and pulled a brown leather over the top. He'd found it in the bottom of the wardrobe, and it was less … challenging … than the black one. More proper.

It was nearly lunchtime and if he was going to do this, now was the time.

Will took a deep breath. The closer he had gotten to The George, the queasier he had felt about it. What if he went in and someone in there just pointed at him, like Donald Sutherland at the end of that film? What if Cherry was there behind the bar and she saw him and screamed? What if the police were waiting in there?

Will shook his head. *Calm the fuck down.*

None of that was going to happen. He was going to walk in. The pub was going to be empty. It was barely twelve. Cherry was going to be behind the bar. She was going to see him and smile. She was going to say *Hello stranger. Long time no see.* And drop her knickers. Well, maybe not *everything* was going to happen just like that. Wishful thinking.

Will smiled. It was going to be fine.

He crossed the street and took one last breath, with his hand on the brass door handle, before pushing it open.

The pub was unchanged. The mess from the other night cleared up, but aside from that, it was the same desolate place from all those months ago. It was somehow different in the daytime, when it was quiet. Cherry was at the bar, pouring a pint. Will glanced at the young guy on one of the stools at the end of the bar—the only other person in there. He had his head down but was watching Cherry. She looked up, a glance, at Will, then poured her attention back on the pint.

She hadn't recognised him. Fair enough. But she would. He walked over to the bar and sat a few feet down from her and waited for her to finish. Cherry finished pouring the pint and carried it to the guy down the far end. They exchanged a few words that Will couldn't hear, and then she turned and came up the bar to Will.

"What'll it be?" she asked.

She looked incredible. Six months without having eyes on her had made her glow. Will smiled. He tried to remember how he would have looked then, only six months ago, but he'd changed so much. Will opened his mouth to speak, but no words came out, instead his lips drifted to a smile. And then she clicked.

"William?"

"Hi," he said, unsure if she was going to kick off over what had happened the other night.

"What happened to you? Where have you been?"

Will internally breathed a sigh of relief. "Around," he said. "Off working. Getting stuff done."

"Here," she took down a bottle of whiskey. The good stuff. And poured a thick shot into a glass. "On the house."

She slid the glass over the bar in front of him and reached down and touched the top of his wrist where some Enochian was poking out of his shirt. "Got some tattoos too?"

Her touch raced electricity up his arm. He wanted to blurt out his intentions, there and then. *Stay calm*. "Yes." The word came out softly. More so than he'd wanted. He cleared his throat.

She smiled, warmly, and let his wrist go. "I'll be back," she said. She walked down to the other guy at the end of the bar and again, exchanged words with him. They seemed quiet, whispered, but that was probably just Will's imagination. He rolled the whiskey around in the glass. Not his usual tipple. But she returned soon enough and stood with him again. "Did you hear about the trouble in here the other night?"

Will raised his eyebrows and shook his head, silent.

"Some thugs fighting. Weirdest thing, too. Danny was on shift, said he told the police all about it. Someone bottled some poor girl in the face and beat someone else half to death. Anyway. Danny said he couldn't remember what the bloke looked like. He told me he was like some dream person."

Will frowned. "Yeah, weird." *Belle*, he thought. She must have done something to keep him safe. Or maybe just to keep herself safe? That didn't make any sense. She could be anything she wanted to be when she was here, and had gone now. If she came back again, she'd probably look like someone else entirely. "Any idea who it was?"

"None. That's the thing. Nobody seemed to remember what the guy looked like. I mean, that's fucking creepy."

Will nodded. He felt a little bad for the way he'd finished things with Belle, now. She was clearly looking after him. "Look," Will said, knocking back the whiskey. "I was just wondering if you wanted to hook up one night?"

"Aren't you the charmer?" Cherry looked a little taken aback. "Hook up?"

Will hadn't meant for it to come out like that. "I'm sorry, I mean—"

"Now if you'd asked me six months ago …" she let her voice drift away. "However, you have been beaten to the finish line. I've already got a date." She looked over her shoulder to the other guy. "For tonight, actually."

Will looked down the bar at him. Both Will and Cherry staring at him must have given him the willies or something because the guy looked up at them. He raised his glass in a toast at the two of them and smiled. "Chin-chin." He put the glass down without taking a sip.

Will stared at him for a moment and then he looked to Cherry. "Who is he?" he asked, his throat tightening as he spoke.

"Name's Bill," she answered. "It's his first time in here today, and won't you look at that. He's already asked me out."

"Bill," Will repeated. *Fucking Bill*. He stared at the guy. *Belle*, he thought. *The fuck*. He tore his attention from *Bill* who hadn't taken his eyes from Will since he had said *chin-fucking-chin*, and looked at Cherry. "Come on, Cherry. How about it? I'll take you somewhere nice."

"Bill said he'd take me somewhere nice."

Will chewed the inside of his cheek. "Don't be so stubborn," he said too loudly.

"Huh," Cherry responded and turned away, storming down the bar and disappearing out the back.

Will shook his head. "For fuck's sake," he whispered. He placed his glass on the bar and rolled it around in his fingers, before letting it go and walking slowly down to the guy sitting on the stool. He slipped up onto the one next to him, looking at him in mirror set into the wall behind the bar. "Bill, huh?"

"Will." Bill nodded.

"Couldn't come up with a better name?"

"Nope."

Bill was a beautiful man, even Will could tell in the mirror. He looked *curated*. Sculpted. He had a jaw, deftly secreted behind a shallow stubble, and piercing blue eyes. His hair was *insta* modelled, his clothes fashionable, but not foppish. "What the fuck are you doing?" Will asked.

Bill smiled, raising his glass into the mirror. "I wanted to know who you dumped me for."

Will let his whole body slump slightly. "But why? I thought you'd be off demoning around someone else by now."

"Nope."

"So what *is* your plan? You've seen. Are you going to fuck off now or what?"

"Nope." Bill slid around on his stool. "Thought

I'd stick around and see what else I could pick up while I'm here."

Cherry returned to the bar from the back and shot a dirty look at Will, now that he'd moved. Bill watched her and smiled.

"No," Will said, dropping his voice to a whisper, well aware that she could hear their conversation now. "You leave her the fuck alone."

"You and what army are going to stop me? I'll get to know her, find out what her demons are, fix them, get a couple of souls along the way, fuck her …" Bill's voice dropped to a whisper so quiet, that Will could barely hear him.

Will sighed. "What do you want?"

"Hm?"

"What do you want to go away?"

"Oh, I don't know. You could have had me until I was bored, and then I would have gone of my own volition. Perhaps this situation wouldn't have occurred." He looked at Will. "Perhaps."

"You want me? Is that it? Come on then. Come home with me now, and I'll forget all about Cherry."

Bill put his hand on Will's knee. "I didn't know you were like that."

Will flicked his hand away. "You know what I mean."

"It doesn't bother you that I am a man currently. If I were Belle you would take me back and fuck me and do all those things to me again, knowing that I am whatever I want to be?"

"I guess I've always known."

Bill looked around the bar. Still empty apart from the three of them. "No cigar." He slid his stool back, scraping it across the floor. "I'll see you at eight, then?" he called over to Cherry.

She looked up and smiled at him. "Eight," she agreed.

Bill tipped his head at Will and smiled, turned and left without further word.

Will looked at Cherry. He knew that there was no point in arguing with her further. Even if she wasn't that keen on *Bill* she was going to dig her heels in just to prove a point. Besides, Bill was stunningly handsome. Will screwed up his face. "Oh for fuck's sake," he said with enough volume for Cherry to hear. He also got up, following Bill out into the street.

He was unsurprised to find Bill gone.

CHAPTER 14

Will stood in the small square park opposite The George. He was wearing a hoodie under his black leather, jeans, and DMs. He had a crowbar in his backpack. His plan—what there was of it—was to rile Belle, or Bill, or Belphegor, or what-the-fuck-ever, into doing something demon-y in front of Cherry. Proving that she shouldn't go out with him. Her mortal soul was at stake.

Even in his head it sounded ridiculous.

He looked at the time. It was nearly eight. It made sense that they would be meeting here. While he hadn't heard them making plans, even Cherry wasn't stupid enough to give out her address, surely.

But what if she had?

Will shook his head. *Don't be stupid. Just wait.*

A couple of minutes past and then Cherry came out of the pub. *Good.* She was dressed sexy. She was obviously planning on a nice night. Hell, who wouldn't with Bill McCooljaw? She was wearing a vintage looking get up that was all the rage these days. She was clutching her handbag in front of her. Will wanted her. He wanted her now. He had to resist leaving the safety of the park after dark to rush over to her, tell her how he felt. *Just wait.*

Thirty seconds to eight and Bill walks around the corner. He was wearing a suit. Slim one. Made him look like he needed to eat some pies. And a bit fucking hipstery. He walked up to her. Fucking hell. They made a good couple. Surely this had to be on purpose?

The two of them embraced quickly, like friends. Polite. Then Bill took Cherry's arm and started to lead her away, across the front of the pub and away from the town centre. Will could hear her giggling in the hush of the evening.

He followed at a distance he deemed to be safe. He had no idea how close he could get to Bill without him knowing he was there. But he hadn't turned. He was just talking to Cherry. He was seducing her.

Will realized how fucking immature he was. All Belle had to do to seduce *him* was turn up naked with beer. It made him hate himself. It made the feelings that he had after the incident all those months ago rise back up in him, a deviant sickness in his gut, the feeling that it was all his fault.

Just like this.

All his fault.

And as much as he hated himself, he hated Bill more. Not for what he had done to him. But for what he was about to do to her. She didn't deserve it. *She wasn't damaged goods.*

Will slipped the backpack from around his shoulder and pulled the crowbar out of it, before slipping it back on over both shoulders. He felt the heft of the iron bar. It was big enough to do some serious damage to that pretty-boy face of his.

Will used his other hand to pull the hood out from

the back of his jacket, and slid it over his head. He wasn't expecting it to provide much in the way of a disguise, but it was better than nothing, he supposed.

Not that he was expecting to make it out of this unscathed anyway. Make the fucker demon out on him, and prove a point. It was probably going to hurt, but it might score him some sweet, sweet, sympathy points with Cherry, once she realized what this butthole was really like.

He continued on behind them as they went further from the town. *Where are they going?* Will carried the iron concealed up his sleeve, as they left the main road and started to cross the park. It didn't matter where they were going, this was the perfect place.

It was dark and empty.

Will waited for them to get a reasonable distance into the park. Cherry was sure to scream. *Sure to*. And Will didn't need any have-a-go-heroes jumping in on the act until it was done.

He followed them, sliding the backpack from his back and letting it drop to the grass silently. He slipped the iron from his sleeve and carried it in his left hand, giving it a couple of swings to make sure he was ready for the hit. Just hard enough to make him show his true self.

The two of them were only feet ahead of him.

Here goes.

Will waited until they seemed to be bumping shoulders. They looked off balance. He took the chance, and charged Bill, shoving him to the ground.

He toppled to the grass, and rolled onto his back.

"What the fuck," Cherry pushed Will by the shoulder. It wasn't hard. It was the sort of shove you'd give a mate on the playground if he was being a cheeky cunt.

Will shoved her back. He didn't mean to push her so hard, but she stumbled backwards onto her arse. He turned his attention to Bill. He was still sitting in the grass, having made no attempt to get back up. He was grinning like a Cheshire fucking cat. Will aimed the iron at him like a blade. "Show her," he shouted. "*Show her.*"

Bill just stared at him.

"Show me what? What the fuck are you talking about?"

Will glanced at Cherry. She was just starting to get to her feet, fighting with the dress. "He's not human," he said, the iron still pointing into Bill face. "He was a she last week."

"What are you taking?" she said.

Will turned his attention back to Bill. Still grinning. Will raised the iron. "Watch," he said.

"*No!*" Cherry screamed.

Will brought the iron down hard on Bill's temple opening him up like a ripe tomato. His face split open, the front of the skull parting from the temple, the skin splitting, and the brain being exposed. Fluid sprayed across Will, and Bill? Bill just sat there. He didn't speak and he didn't move, his smile plastered on his face like a wax work. "Say something, you cunt." Will brought the iron back down, cleaving a gash into Bill's broken face. His eye caving in, black fluid spewing down his face. His head jarred to the left and his body flopped onto its side, brain and bone slopping lazily onto the grass. "Do something." Will brought it up and down for a third time, this time caving the top of his head in.

Then there was pain. A warm tingling that started on his hip, radiating outwards until an explosion erupted in his side. Will looked down. He couldn't see anything. What had Bill done? Then he saw Cherry. She was standing there behind him. She had something in her hand.

It glinted in the moonlight.

A blade.

She'd fucking stabbed him.

She was crying. "Stop it," she wailed. Then she thrust forward with the blade again, straight into Will's gut.

Fuck.

He recoiled backwards, slipping off the blade and to the grass. Letting go of the iron, he rested his hand on his stomach. It hurt, and was weirdly numb at the same time. The warmth of his blood slopping over his skin felt good against the sudden coldness of his fingers. *I'm bleeding out*, he thought. He looked to the side, to Bill still laying in the grass, his face a mash of bone fragments and fluids, clear, black, and red. His one good eye staring at him. That smile on his face still.

Will found everything starting to go black. He was sure his eyes weren't closing. It was just getting darker. As he stared, Bill winked at him through the bloody mess of his skull. As least, Will thought he had.

Maybe it was just a trick of his own mind as the blood that should have been in his brain was keeping his hands warm.

Maybe that was it.

About the Author

Ash is a British horror author. He resides in the south, in the Garden of England. He writes horror that is sometimes fantastical, sometimes grounded, but always deeply graphic, and black with humour.

Printed in Great Britain
by Amazon